whenever there is danger, send for...

Kung Fu
Pigs

ISBN 0-439-62646-3

12 11 10 9 8 7 6 5 4 3 2   4 5 6 7 8 9/0

Printed in the U.S.A.   40
First Scholastic printing, April 2004

Kung Fu pigs

Hostages of the Jade Wolf

Keith Brumpton

SCHOLASTIC INC.

New York Toronto London Auckland Sydney
Mexico City New Delhi Hong Kong Buenos Aires

THE LO-FAT HILLS

THE CAVE
WITH
NO NAME
Home of the Cr

CHIN CHIN
(Rinki's home)

PORKAIDO

KNOCKNEEDO

The Pork-i Kingdom

BRIDGE OF THE
SEVENTH GOLDFISH

NO-PEKIN
Capital city, home to
our great and noble emperor

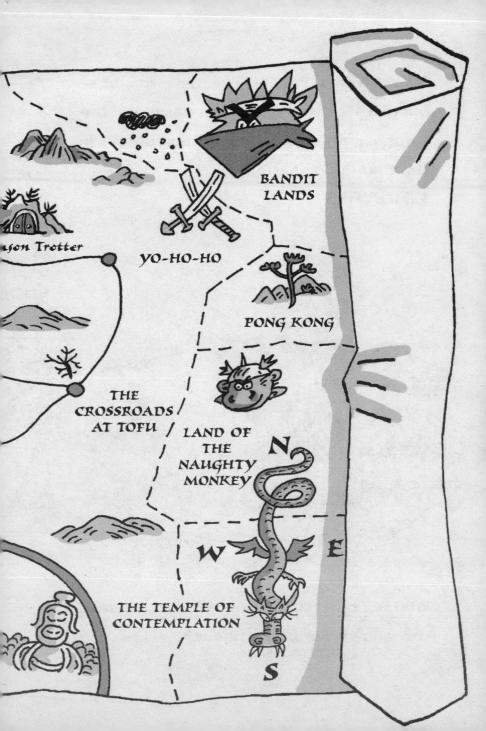

For centuries, Pig and Wolf have fought — but with a new young emperor on the throne, perhaps peace will reign at last in the Pork-i kingdom?

WRONG!!!

Who will protect the boy emperor against the wolfish hordes? Anyone?

Forces of war
and disorder

Hostages of the Jade Wolf

Translated from the original Pork-i manuscript by Keith Brumpton

PROLOGUE

I am the old and wise Oinky No Ho, venerable priest of Wu-Dah-Ling, and this is the story of how the Kung Fu Pigs, those determined defenders of the emperor, came into being. It is a story in which I myself have a small part to play.

At the time, as you will probably recall, the young Emperor Ping-Pong had just ascended to the throne (with some difficulty, because he only had short legs). All was not well in our land. That evil traitor, the Crimson Trotter, was stirring up trouble on our borders. Bandits ransacked our villages, and no one could feel safe. The emperor himself was too weak and too young to do much about all this. Was there anyone who could help him in this, his hour of need? Let us see . . .

CHAPTER 1

*"An old heart may be heavy, but a
young heart knows no fear."*
Proverb, Te-He province

Imagine, if you will, the peaceful village of
Chin Chin one fine June morning.
Spring was coming to an end,
and the last of the
cherry blossoms
had fallen from the
trees like
snow.

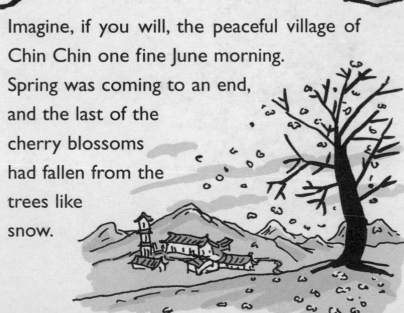

But things weren't as peaceful as they seemed. For in this small village, the locals were living in fear. At night, their little hooves knocked together like castanets. And what was it exactly that had struck terror into the hearts of these simple country pigs? Be patient and all will be revealed!

First we must meet a young pig of noble birth, also living in that troubled village. His name was Rinki, and he was a kung fu expert, the finest for many a mile despite his young age. I know because I know the old master who taught him.

One day, the village innkeeper came to Rinki, his eyes filled with tears.

"What's the matter?" asked Rinki, guessing from his tears that the old pig was either very troubled or had recently been chopping onions. The innkeeper tried to stifle his sobs.

"The J-Jade Wolf — that most fearsome bandit from the Lo-Fat Hills! He and his g-gang have t-taken my wife and son hostage!"

"Hostage?" gasped Rinki.

"Yes. That's when someone takes someone else prisoner until you pay them a large sum of money."

"I know what a hostage is," snapped Rinki irritably, for he was a young and impatient pig.

The innkeeper showed Rinki the ransom note and then asked if he could help find his family. Rinki didn't have to think for long. He had always longed for adventure, and now he'd found it!

"Very well, Yu-Hu," he replied (for that was the innkeeper's name).

Your money or your wife! If you want to see your old lady and the kid again, then be prepared to fork out. You'll hear from me soon.

Yours criminally,
Jade Wolf

"I'll try to find your wife and son. But how will I recognize them?"

Yu-Hu described his wife and son to Rinki. He described them in such detail that Rinki felt as though he knew them. And then he remembered that he *did* know them. They lived next door.

Rinki wasted no time. Within minutes he was striding off down the narrow road that led out of the village. He carried with him a staff made from bamboo and a sack filled with rice crackers. The old innkeeper stood and waved until our young hero was out of sight and heading toward the Lo-Fat Hills, home to bandits, wolves, and all manner of evil spirits.

CHAPTER 2

"A journey is always farther than the lines on the map."
Proverb, Sun-Fun, philosopher

Rinki made good progress along the dusty road. His young legs were strong and his snout was filled with the smell of adventure.

As dusk fell, he saw that he could go no farther, for the night — as usual in these parts — was dark. He lit a fire by rubbing twigs together, and sat warming himself by the flames.

But what Rinki didn't know (for he was a young pig of little experience) was that one should never light an open fire when in bandit country. Better to shiver with cold than to attract the unwelcome attention of those villains who prey upon the lonely traveler . . .

wolves . . .

bandits . . .

. . . heavily armed sheep.

Rinki made himself a simple bed from dried grass and the last of the rice crackers. It was noisy but surprisingly comfortable, and before long, our young hero had settled into a peaceful slumber.

"Sleep not little pig, when bandits are at hand!"

Had Rinki forgotten the wise words of his master? Yes, I'm afraid he had. And before too long, the sound of his peaceful snoring reached the ears of a group of bandits returning to their hideout. (Bandits always have good hearing.)

Rinki continued to doze on his makeshift bed, dreaming of brave deeds and kung fu daring-do. And all the while, the bandits crept ever closer.

Suddenly, Rinki felt something against his ribs. He thought at first it was a squirrel. But squirrels don't wear riding boots, not in these parts, anyway.

Rinki reached for his bamboo staff, but it wasn't there. Seconds later, he felt firm, furry wolf-paws holding him tightly.

"Unhand me at once!" he shouted, but his demand was met only with laughter. Four bandits encircled our hero. The bandit leader picked up Rinki's bag and emptied its contents onto the ground.

"I have no gold!" honked the young pig, still trying to free himself.

"Then all the worse for you!" laughed the bandit chief, whose name was Dum Song. He told his cronies to take Rinki to the river and throw him in.

And that might have been the end of our hero had something not happened to change events, just as a small pebble in a river can sometimes alter the course of a whole stream.

CHAPTER 3

"The sky has to be black before we can see the stars."
Emperor He-Be-Je-Be, 3rd century

"Ahhhhhhh-sohhhhhhh!"

A large samurai pig somersaulted into the circle of bandits.

Dum Song swung around with a snarl on his crooked, wolfish lips. "So — someone else wants to join the country oinker for a swim?"

The samurai pig, whose name was Stinki, gave no answer, but drew his bow. Some of the bandits already looked a little worried, for they were more used to stealing from the weak and weary traveler than taking on a fully armed samurai pig.

"Eeeowwww!"

Stinki flipped himself high into the air with all the athleticism of a circus flea. In a flurry of bamboo and hooves, he dealt with two of the bandits with a single blow.

The third bandit fled into the bushes with a whimper, dropping his sword as he ran.

Stinki stood laughing, thinking that the battle was won, but the bandit chief was made of sterner stuff than his fellow wolves. In an instant, Dum Song drew his sword and ran toward Stinki. The samurai pig had no time to react; Dum Song's sword split his bamboo staff in two as though it were a noodle. The bandit's sharp white teeth flashed a gloating smile. Now it was the samurai pig who was defenseless.

But before the bandit could strike again, Rinki leaped through the air and felled the wolf with an expert kung fu "Haiko." His hooves began to deal a blur of lightning-fast blows. Dum Song didn't stand a chance.

In minutes, the struggle was over, and Dum Song had fled after the rest of his gang.

Stinki breathed a sigh of relief. "Thank you, stranger," he honked, bowing low. "Nice work."

"And thank you, noble samurai," replied Rinki. "Will you join me for some supper? I believe those wolves left their provisions behind in their hurry to escape."

"Oh, yes," answered Stinki. "I'm absolutely starving!"

And so it was that the two pigs roasted a fat carp by the fire and talked long into the night as though they were old friends.

CHAPTER 4

"A good friendship is like a good cooking pot: You should carry it everywhere."
Sho-Mi-Da-Wei, poet, Dong Dynasty

Morning broke over the distant blue hills, and Rinki woke remembering his mission to rescue the innkeeper's wife and child.

Stinki was cooking a huge breakfast over a crackling campfire. After their meal, Stinki said he would walk with his new friend as far as the forest. As they walked, they continued to talk, as pigs will.

Stinki listened with excitement to the story of the innkeeper and how Jade Wolf's bandits were holding his family hostage.

"I'd like to accompany you on that quest! You're too young to take on a whole gang on your own, especially a gang led by Jade Wolf! You need someone else — someone who doesn't mind a fight!"

Rinki was only too glad to accept the offer. The samurai pig was a fine fighter and good company, even if he did talk about food all the time.

Later that day, when they came to the forest, the hearts of our two pig heroes suddenly grew heavy, for they knew that a place so full of darkness might well be home to demons or evil spirits. On the other hand, of course, it might just be full of trees.

"I don't like this at all," said Stinki as they walked on. "Is there no other way to reach the bandits' hideout?"

Rinki shook his head. "Turn back if you wish, Stinki. It is only I who made a promise to the old innkeeper."

Stinki's eyes were suddenly as steely as his samurai armor. "A samurai pig never returns to his trough until the task is done! On my honor, we will see this through."

So the two pigs continued deep into the forest. The footpath had almost vanished, and tall pine trees grew overhead in twisted, frightening shapes. Rinki thought they resembled great black serpents.

As they walked, Stinki thought he heard a strange rustling from the bushes. He drew his bow nervously and turned his head, expecting to see some terrifying spirit armed to the teeth with sword and spear. But there, instead, stood a beautiful young piglet dressed in a simple silk blouse, typical of the region.

"Welcome, strangers," she said, making a low bow. How nice to see a pig with good manners!

A strange, ghostly wind, like the sound of an out-of-tune flute, blew through the trees wherever the young girl piglet walked. Was she enchanted?

Stinki certainly thought so, for he was at heart a simple country pig, who believed in magic spirits and suchlike.

The newcomer sat down in the shade of a tall pine tree and took out a fine porcelain bowl.

"I have with me some green tea," she continued. "Will you share it?"

The two travelers nodded eagerly, for they hadn't stopped to drink or eat since morning. And for Stinki, especially, that was a very long time.

"Thank you, young lady. I don't suppose you have anything to eat as well?"

Rinki gave his friend a sharp dig in the ribs.

CHAPTER 5

*"The trees may seem silent,
but listen for the trunk call."*
Jet Pak, 2nd century

Stinki had drunk greedily from the blue porcelain bowl the piglet had presented them with and then passed it to Rinki. The tea seemed refreshing, but oddly appeared only to make our friends grow more sleepy.

As Rinki looked up, the trees seemed to close in on him, like a green army. He had a funny feeling that all was not well, but his eyes felt heavy — too heavy to stay open. Stinki the samurai already lay snoring next to him.

And what about the young piglet with the silk blouse and cute pigtails? Of her there was no sign. Instead, the sleepy Rinki saw an evil forest spirit hovering over him. A tall, terrifying creature with large fangs and long, sharp claws. It was only then that he realized they had been tricked. The tea was not tea at all, but a sleeping potion. And the pretty young piglet was not a pretty young piglet at all.

It is a power of the evil spirits that they can transform themselves into anything they like: a twittering bird, an animal cracker, a beautiful piglet maiden. So beware — next time you walk through that strange, dark forest, things might not be quite what they seem!

 39

By now the evil spirit had wrapped Rinki and Stinki in a fishing net. Rinki wanted to struggle, but his legs felt as heavy as the old iron bells in Wu-Dah-Ling Monastery.

So our hero could do nothing but watch with frightened eyes as the spirit began preparing a large cooking pot. This was a spirit who liked the taste of fine food, and she wanted to enjoy the two pigs with fresh spices and sauce, cooked in her favorite stew.

The smell of cooking woke Stinki from his sleep. His eyes grew wide with alarm when he saw the situation they were in.

"It has been nice knowing you, Rinki," began the samurai pig. "Looks like we won't be finishing our mission."

"It's not over yet," muttered Rinki through gritted teeth. For did his master not teach him that a great warrior never gives in, not even when all seems lost?

The evil forest spirit sipped the sauce now sizzling in the pot and licked her grizzly lips. Now was the time to add the final two ingredients: Rinki and Stinki!

CHAPTER 6

"The wise pig never laughs when another tries to fly."
Anonymous

At about the same time as our two friends were heading for the pot, a young pig from the village of Ho Ho was making her way to a distant monastery where she was to study. Her route took her through the same dark forest where our heroes were held captive.

Dinki (for that was her name) hurried along the sandy path strewn with pine needles and leaves. Her parents had warned her of this forest, and she knew it was home to evil spirits.

Dinki was a very smart young pig, the smartest in her village. Smarter even than Dim-Doh, the village elder, who claimed he could count up to one hundred.

So when she smelled the spices and sweet-and-sour sauce, she knew that something — or someone — was destined for the cooking pot!

And when she looked down into the soft sand of the path, she could see quite clearly the imprint of pig hooves. Two sets.

"Some fellow pigs are in danger! But I'll be in danger, too, if I linger for too long in this dangerous place."

And then another thought came into her head. "As a priestess, is it not my duty to help others?"

Now she was confused, like a dragon with two tails.

And while Dinki dithered on the dusty road, the sweet-and-sour sauce had come to a boil and the evil spirit was just about to dine!

"Better to start with the young noble-pig," thought the spirit to herself. "That samurai looks like he might be a bit tough."

And so saying, she was just about to pick up young Rinki and put him into the pot when the sound of someone rushing through the undergrowth distracted her for a moment. A bamboo staff spun like a wheel. Black pigtails whistled in the wind.

And there stood Dinki, the priestess, armed with her simple bamboo staff.

The evil spirit looked at Dinki, now standing before her, dressed in a pale gold dress and simple clogs.

"Who are you?" the spirit snorted. "Dessert?"

Dinki's eyes flashed with defiance. She may have been short in stature, but she wasn't short of courage. She took up her fighting position: "Pig Facing West."

"Run!" shouted Rinki and Stinki, watching from afar. "Save yourself!"

But even when the evil spirit took out her bow and drew herself up to her full height, Dinki the priestess showed no signs of turning pig-tail.

CHAPTER 7

"The tiger prefers to sleep than to fight, but when the time comes, he will do it, tooth and claw."
Ho-Chi-Chin, 1st century

In these troubled times, when the Crimson Trotter threatens our emperor and gangs of robber wolves roam the land, no pig is safe in his or her own sty. This is why even peaceful monks and priestesses have learned how to defend themselves.

And young Dinki had been well taught by her masters, the Monk Pigs of the Leaky Temple.

From them she had learned the art of "Open Trotter Defense," as well as how to fight with sword and staff and bow. But would this be enough when faced with an evil forest spirit, its long sharp claws now gleaming in the gloom?

Dinki attacked first, for the wise old monks had taught her that "surprise is the sharpest weapon in a pig's armory." Before the evil spirit could react, Dinki leaped high into the branches of an overhanging tree. She drew herself upright, ready for the "Three Stork Shuffle."

"Ahhh-soooohhh!"

Rinki and Stinki stared, openmouthed.

Tching!

Dinki's hooves shattered the evil spirit's bow!

Thwack! Now Dinki's staff broke into three pieces!

The gloomy forest echoed sounds of conflict. But it seemed that the spirit still had the upper hand. Her eyes gleamed hungrily at the thought of the feast to come— three courses now, instead of two.

Rinki and Stinki watched in horror as Dinki was knocked to the ground. The spirit licked her lips and advanced on Dinki.

"Poor kid," sighed Rinki.

"She should have run when we told her," said Stinki. "Kids these days just don't listen."

Suddenly, Dinki rolled over to one side and onto her hooves. With a spell she'd learned in her own monastery, she conjured her fighting staff back together. Three pieces of broken bamboo suddenly became one again.

And before the devilish spirit could react, she struck the evil creature right between the eyes. (This is just the place to strike a forest spirit, should you ever need to.)

In an instant, the vile monster had shattered into pieces like a lump of old, damp firewood.

Rinki and Stinki couldn't believe their eyes. It was only when the young priestess freed them from the fishing net and started to untie their ropes that they knew, against all odds, they'd been rescued!

CHAPTER 8

"The searcher for truth must climb every mountain and ford every stream."
Chu-Li-Andrews, 3rd century

Leaving behind the bewitched forest, the three pigs now climbed the long and winding road that led to the Lo-Fat Hills, for the priestess Dinki had agreed to join our friends until their paths parted. All through the afternoon, the three travelers swapped stories and songs.

After a while, they got to talking about Rinki's mission to rescue the innkeeper's wife and child, held captive by the bandits of the Lo-Fat Hills.

"You really know how to handle yourself, Dinki," began Stinki. "Why don't you help us with our mission, too?"

Dinki gave a modest smile.

"Your cause is a good one, fellow pigs, but I was taught by my master only to use my kung fu in order to protect myself."

Rinki and Dinki looked disappointed but said no more on the subject — they could see that the pigtailed priestess's mind was already made up. The three pigs continued on their way, and it was a difficult walk, for the Lo-Fat Hills were very hilly and not particularly low.

"How much farther?" grumbled Stinki. "My stomach is empty and my hooves are aching."

Rinki, being the leader, tried hard to pretend he wasn't feeling exhausted, too. He forged ahead, encouraging the others as best he could. But suddenly, something whizzed through the air, right past his ear, causing him to duck down low.

When he turned back toward Stinki, he saw his friend lying sprawled on the ground.

"Get down!" yelled Stinki at the top of his voice. Rinki glimpsed an arrow, still quivering in the trunk of a nearby tree, and realized they were under attack.

"Bandits!" whispered Dinki, crouching down beside her friends. The young priestess was right. A gang of bandit wolves had begun to move through the trees toward them, armed to the teeth. And what long, dangerous teeth they were, too!

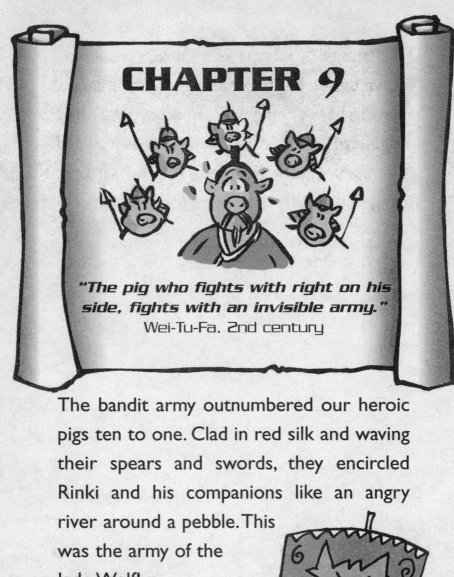

CHAPTER 9

"The pig who fights with right on his side, fights with an invisible army."
Wei-Tu-Fa, 2nd century

The bandit army outnumbered our heroic pigs ten to one. Clad in red silk and waving their spears and swords, they encircled Rinki and his companions like an angry river around a pebble. This was the army of the Jade Wolf!

"Come and do your worst!" shouted Stinki, defiantly. He stood in his "Crane" position, one leg raised and the other anchored on the ground, and then sent two of the bandits reeling.

Dinki, meanwhile, somersaulted backward, out of sight, though not before she, too, had dealt with a couple of the bandits. The luckless wolves were knocked off the path and into a clump of prickly bushes. At the same time, Rinki's hooves were flashing like swords, and none of the bandits could match him for long.

Seeing his bandit army in such disarray, their leader, Jade Wolf, rode into view and dismounted from a fine horse. The horse was black, like Jade Wolf's heart. The bandit leader himself was a terrifying figure. Taller by far than any of his followers and with great gleaming fangs, Jade Wolf was feared by all who knew him. Living a life of luxury in an abandoned temple, he bowed to no one, not even the emperor!

"Did he have a bad back?" I hear you ask. "Is that why he didn't bow?" No — he didn't have a bad back, just a bad attitude.

And now there he stood, sword drawn, fangs bared, ready to challenge our heroes.

It was Rinki who first leaped forward to face the bandit chief. In his mind, he was remembering his master's instructions: "Avoid the fight. Use words as your sword."

And so Rinki called out: "Throw down your weapons, Jade Wolf! Return your captives and depart in peace!"

The bandit leader stood silent for a moment, as though considering the offer.

But in an instant, his expression changed, and he looked at him with fierce eyes.

"Forget it, impudent youth! Jade Wolf is not about to surrender to three little pigs!" He walked forward, menacingly.

Rinki felt his cheeks grow pink with rage. "OK. Well, don't say I didn't give you a chance!"

He called on his two companions to try to hold off the rest of the bandit army while he took on their leader. And then he rushed toward Jade Wolf, hooves flashing like the spokes of a wheel, every muscle poised for action.

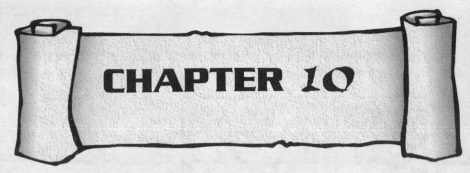

CHAPTER 10

It was quite a fight. The wolf had strength . . .

. . . the pig, speed of thought.

Perhaps that is why the contest lasted so long.

They battled their way up the steps of the old monastery, overgrown with moss.

They danced in and out of the carved statues of Buddha.

They tumbled down onto the pebbled courtyard. Rinki struggled against his wolfish foe. He knew his bamboo staff would not be enough against such an opponent. He reached for his sword.

A clash of metal rang out above the tinkle of a peaceful fountain and the snoring of the palace goldfish as the two swords met.

Sensing his advantage as Jade Wolf seemed to tire, Rinki launched a "Five Tiger" offensive . . .

. . . and knocked Jade Wolf to the ground!

SURRENDER!

cried Rinki, triumphant at last.
"Very well." The bandit
nodded and began
to bow in
surrender.

As Rinki bowed back, the wily Jade Wolf suddenly grabbed a handful of pebbles from the garden and threw them into his young adversary's eyes.

Before Rinki could recover, the treacherous bandit took a flying leap down the monastery steps and up onto his horse.

Rinki tried to block his escape route, but even he could not outrun a swift stallion.

With a howl of defiance, Jade Wolf and his horse were gone!

With their leader defeated, the rest of the bandit gang quickly lost heart. Stinki and Dinki forced them back, step-by-step, until at last their ranks broke. Dinki chased a great pack of them back down the crumbling monastery steps, while Stinki started to search the ruins for any sign of the innkeeper's wife and child.

To find out what happened next, you must hurry to the next chapter just as surely as Jade Wolf's horse hurried to the distant paddy fields.

CHAPTER 11

*"After winter comes the spring,
and finally, the flower."*
No Wei, 2nd Dynasty

Yu-Hu's wife and son were being held prisoner in an old stable. It was Stinki who found them, huddled together beneath a bale of straw, and at first they wouldn't speak because they were too frightened.

This samurai pig who stood before them with his black armor and towering helmet looked every bit as frightening as the bandits who had first captured them!

But when Rinki and Dinki showed up, the captives finally realized they were safe at last. How they celebrated! How great was their joy! They were as happy as pigs in mud. Maybe because they *were* pigs in mud.

"Night is falling," said Rinki when the celebrations were done.

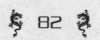

"Is that why it's dark?" asked the innkeeper's wife, who wasn't the brightest snout at the trough.

"Yes." Rinki nodded. "It will be too dangerous to travel back through the woods tonight. We must stay here till dawn."

The innkeeper's wife drew closer to Rinki.

"I have something to show you."

If Rinki had a weakness — and we all have one or two, do we not? — it was his curiosity. So while Dinki and Stinki were looking after little Ho-ki, the innkeeper's son, Rinki was led up the garden path by Yu-Hu's wife, to where an old summer house stood, covered in weeds and eerily lit by an autumn moon. It was a spooky-looking spot.

"This is where those wolves stored their treasure," she whispered to Rinki when she was certain that no one had followed them. "It is filled to the rafters with silver and gold, the finest silks, rugs, and this nice mug with a cute dog on it."

A wicked gleam stole into her eyes. "All this could be ours! We could stay here and live like the emperor himself! In total luxury! We would want for nothing!"

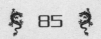

Was Rinki tempted? Did he waver for a moment? No! He turned toward his companion, eyes flashing angrily in the moonlight: "In the first place, these things don't belong to us. And in the second, your husband, the innkeeper, is waiting for you and your son to return home. It is he who sent me here to rescue you!"

The innkeeper's wife looked a little guilty now.

"This evil treasure horde has cast a spell on you," said Rinki. "We must leave at once!"

He turned on his hooves and hurried back down the path.

So it was that even as the moon began to rise, Rinki and his companions and the innkeeper's wife and son set out for home. The woods would be dark and dangerous, but not so dangerous, Rinki concluded, as staying where they were.

Stinki and Dinki would not hear of their friend traveling without them, which is why they agreed to return to Chin Chin together.

And when at last they reached that same village, you can imagine the tears that were shed. Well, maybe you can't, so let me tell you: Whole rivers of joy were cried by the old innkeeper when he saw his family back safe once more.

Dear old Yu-Hu shook our hero's hoof and then slapped him several times on the back.

"Oh, noble young pig, I chose well in my hour of need!"

Rinki smiled modestly. "I did what I could, and couldn't have done even that without the help of my friends, Dinki and Stinki."

He felt a little sad now — sad that his adventure had come to an end. And sad that Dinki would continue on her journey,

and that Stinki would set forth once more in search of new battles to fight and new pies to eat.

Rinki imagined his own life would soon return to those long, tiresome days when nothing much ever

happened. But in thinking this, he was wrong.

Far away, in his magnificent palace, the young emperor, Ping-Pong, heard tales of the exploits of the three little pigs, and of how they had defeated the evil bandit Jade Wolf. The emperor was impressed.

And it took a lot to impress the emperor, for he was, in truth, a rather spoiled young pig.

So it was that within three days a messenger had arrived in the village of Chin Chin and asked to be taken at once to the home of that great and noble warrior pig, Rinki the Wolf-Fighter.

When Rinki read the message from the emperor, his eyes grew wide with astonishment (well, wide for a pig's eyes, which are not, on the whole, very wide at all). The emperor had commanded him, together with the priestess Dinki and Stinki the samurai, to work together to help protect his empire against anyone who might threaten it.

He also said that he wanted them to study with a wise old pig, a master of the ancient kung fu arts, known as Oinky No Ho. Rinki had heard of the noble Oinky, and his heart quickened at the thought of all the skills he might learn with such a wise teacher.

And so it was that Rinki, Dinki, and Stinki made their way to the palace of the great emperor with Ping-Pong's messenger.

Ah, how fine was Ping-Pong's palace! What gold around the throne room, what comfy cushions!

They noticed an elderly pig with long, white whiskers and a shiny bald head who sat next to the emperor. This must be their new master, the learned Oinky No Ho. He was an off-white belt, the highest in the kung fu order.

Our three heroes bowed low and waited for the young emperor, His Royal Piginess, to speak.

"You have done well," squeaked Ping-Pong. "My archenemy, that vile traitor, the Crimson Trotter, will have learned of your brave actions and even now will be trembling at his trough!"

Rinki bowed humbly. The emperor paused for a moment while a courtier dabbed a drop of sweat from his brow.

"Henceforth, I command that the three of you — Rinki, Dinki, and Stinki — be known as the Kung Fu Pigs. And that you be ready for action whenever I summon you. There is a gong in the garden of my learned Oinky No Ho's residence. Whenever this gong sounds, you must hurry at once to my palace."

Rinki smiled with pride, and the Kung Fu Pigs bowed low in acceptance of the emperor's command.

EPILOGUE

So it was that the Kung Fu Pigs became my pupils. You have met them and learned how they rescued the innkeeper's wife and child (who, by the way, are now living peacefully in mud).

If you would like to know more about their adventures, then you must ask elsewhere, for I, Oinky No Ho, have come to the end of this particular pig's tale.

Go in peace, honorable stranger.

Strengths
- Daring
- Agile
- Bold
- A master of the sword
- Fearless

Weaknesses
- Impulsiveness
- Headstrong
- Curiosity

Favorite moves
- The Two-Dragon Slice
- The Celestial Panda Chop
- The Flying Wind Arrow

Strengths

Strength

Courage

Loyalty

A great fighter with all weapons,
especially the bow

Weaknesses

Easily distracted by thoughts of food

Clumsy

Slow to work things out

Favorite moves

Thundering Goldfish Fright

Mad Dragon Charge

Bouncing Rabbit Kick

Murderous Monkey Antagonism

Strengths

- Clarity of thought
- Intelligence
- Coolness under pressure
- Skill with fighting staff

Weaknesses

- Uncommunicative
- Aloof
- Desire to always be right

Favorite moves

- Peaceful Cat Forehead
- Blind Tiger Defense
- The Flying Pigtail Pounce
- Supernatural Mist Touch

The sayings of

Oinky No Ho

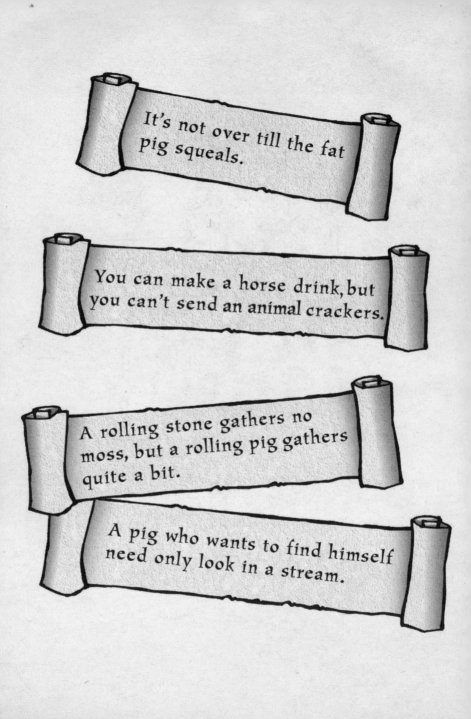

It's not over till the fat pig squeals.

You can make a horse drink, but you can't send an animal crackers.

A rolling stone gathers no moss, but a rolling pig gathers quite a bit.

A pig who wants to find himself need only look in a stream.

A pig with a stick is worth two with a bush.

The pen is mightier than the sword, but the sword is better for chopping onions.

The pig who truly knows himself gets an extra present on feast days.